THE
WORSHIPPERS

THE WORSHIPPERS
Damon Knight

ÆGYPAN PRESS

This story was first published in the March, 1953, issue of
Space Science Fiction.

Special thanks to Greg Weeks, Stephen Blundell, and the
Online Distributed Proofreading Team (which can be found
at http://www.pgdp.net).

The Worshippers
A publication of
ÆGYPAN PRESS

www.aegypan.com

Destiny reached out a hand to Algernon Weaver — but he was a timid man, at first. But on the strange world of Terranova, there was much to be learned — of destiny, and other things. . . .

I

*I*t was a very different thing, Algernon Weaver decided, actually to travel in space. When you read about it, or thought about it in terms of what you read, it was more a business of going from one name to another. Algol to Sirius. Aldebaran to Epsilon Ceti. You read the names, and the descriptions that went with them, and the whole thing — although breathtaking in concept, of course, when you really stopped to *meditate* on it — became rather ordinary and prosaic and somehow more understandable.

Not that he had ever approved. No. He had that, at least, to look back upon; he had seen the whole enterprise as pure presumption, and had said so. Often. The heavens were the heavens, and Earth was Earth. It would have been better — *much* better for all concerned — if it had been left that way.

He had held that opinion, he reminded himself gratefully, from the very beginning, when it was easy to think otherwise. Afterward, of course — when the first star ships came back with the news that space was aswarm with creatures who did not even resemble Man, and had never heard of him, and did not think much of him when they saw him. . . . Well, who but an idiot could hold any other opinion?

If only the Creator had not seen fit to make so many human beings in His image but without His common sense. . . .

Well, if He hadn't then for one thing, Weaver would not have been where he was now, staring out an octagonal porthole at an endless sea of diamond-pierced blackness, with the empty ship humming to itself all around him.

*I*t was an entirely different thing, he told himself; there were no names, and no descriptions, and no feeling of going from one known place to another known place. It was more like —

It was like standing outdoors, on a still summer night, and looking up at the dizzying depths of the stars. And then looking down, to discover that there was no planet under your feet — and that you were all alone in that alien gulf. . . .

It was enough to make a grown man cry; and Weaver had cried, often, in the empty red twilight of the ship, feeling himself hopelessly and forever cut off, cast out and forgotten. But as the weeks passed, a kind of numbness had overtaken him, till now, when he looked out the porthole at the incredible depth of sky, he felt no emotion but a thin, disapproving regret.

Sometimes he would describe himself to himself, just to refute the feeling that he was not really here, not really alive. But his mind was too orderly, and the description would come out so cold and terse — "Algernon James Weaver (1942–) historian, civic leader, poet, teacher, philosopher. Author of *Development of the School System in Schenectady and Schoharie Counties, New York* (pamphlet, 1975); *An Address to the Women's Clubs of Schenectady, New York* (pamphlet, 1979); *Rhymes of a Philosopher* (1981); *Parables of a Philosopher* (1983), *Reflections of a Philosopher* (1986). Born in Detroit, Michigan, son of a Methodist minister; educated in Michigan and New York public schools; B.A., New York State University, 1959; M.A., N.Y.S.U. Extension, 1964. Unmarried. Surviving relatives —"

That was the trouble, it began to sound like an obituary. And then the great humming metal shell would begin to feel like a coffin. . . .

Presumption. Pure presumption. None of these creatures should have been allowed to get loose among the stars, Man least of all. It cluttered up the Universe. It undermined Faith. And it had got Algernon Weaver into the devil of a fix.

*I*t was his sister's fault, actually. She would go, in spite of his advice, up to the Moon, to the UN sanatorium in Aristarchus. Weaver's sister, a big-framed, definite woman, had a weak heart and seventy-five superfluous pounds of fat. Doctors had told her that she would live twenty years longer on the Moon; therefore she went, and survived the trip, and thrived in the germ-free atmosphere, weighing just one-sixth of her former two hundred and ten pounds.

Once, she was there, Weaver could hardly escape visiting her. Harriet was a widow, with large resources, and Weaver was her only near relative. It was necessary,

it was prudent, for him to keep on her good side.
Moreover, he had his family feeling.

He did not like it, not a minute of it. Not the
incredible trip, rising till the Earth lay below like a
botched model of itself; not the silent mausoleum of
the Moon. But he duly admired Harriet's spacious room
in the sanatorium, the recreation rooms, the audito-
rium; space-suited, he walked with her in the cold
Earthlight; he attended her on the excursion trip to Ley
Field, the interstellar rocket base on the far side of the
Moon.

The alien ship was there, all angles and planes
— it came from Zeta Aurigae, they told him, and was
the second foreign ship to visit Sol. Most of the crew
had been ferried down to Earth, where they were inspecting the people (without approval, Weaver was
sure). Meanwhile, the remaining crewman would be
pleased to have the sanatorium party inspect *him*.

*T*hey went aboard, Harriet and two other women,
and six men counting the guide and Weaver. The ship
was a red-lit cavern. The "crewman" turned out to be a
hairy horror, a three-foot headless lump shaped like an

eggplant, supported by four splayed legs and with an indefinite number of tentacles wriggling below the stalked eyes.

"They're more like us than you'd think," said the guide. "They're mammals, they have a nervous organization very like ours, they're susceptible to some of our diseases — which is very rare — and they even share some of our minor vices." He opened his kit and offered the thing a plug of chewing tobacco, which was refused with much tentacle-waving, and a cigar, which was accepted. The creature stuck the cigar into the pointed tip of its body, just above the six beady black eyes, lit it with some sort of flameless lighter, and puffed clouds of smoke like a volcano.

"— And of course, as you see, they're oxygen breathers," the guide finished. "The atmosphere in the ship here is almost identical to our own — we could breathe it without any discomfort whatever."

Then why don't we? Weaver thought irritably. He had been forced to wear either a breathing mask or a pressure suit all the time he had been on the Moon, except when he had been in his own sealed room at the sanatorium. And his post-nasal drip was unmistakably maturing into a cold; he had been stifling sneezes for the last half hour.

He was roused by a commotion up ahead; someone was on the floor, and the others were crowding around. "Help me carry her," said the guide's voice sharply in his earphones. "We can't treat her here. What is she, a heart case?. . . Good Lord. Clear the way there, will you?"

Weaver hurried up, struck by a sharp suspicion. Indeed, it was Harriet who was being carried out — and a good thing, he thought, that they didn't have to support her full weight. He wondered vaguely if she would die before they got her to a doctor. He could not give the thought his full attention, or feel as much fraternal anxiety as he ought, because —

He had . . . he *had* to sneeze.

*T*he others had crowded out into the red-lit space of the control room, where the airlock was. Weaver stopped and frantically tugged his arm free of the rubberoid sleeve. The repressed spasm was an acute agony in his nose and throat. He fumbled the handkerchief out of his pocket, thrust his hand up under the helmet — and blissfully let go.

His eyes were watering. He wiped them hurriedly, put the handkerchief away, worked his arm back into the sleeve, and looked around to see what had become of the others.

The airlock door was closed, and there was no one in the room but the hairy eggplant shape of the Aurigean, still puffing its cigar.

"Hey!" said Weaver, forgetting his manners. The Aurigean did not turn — but then, which was its front, or back? The beady black eyes regarded him without expression.

Weaver started forward. He got nearly to the airlock before a cluster of hairy tentacles barred his way. He said indignantly, "Let me out, you monster. Let me out, do you hear?"

The creature stood stock-still in an infuriating attitude until a little light on the wall changed from orange to red-violet. Then it crossed to the control board, did something there, and the inner door of the lock swung open.

"Well, I should think so!" said Weaver. He stepped forward again — But his eyes were beginning to water. There was an intolerable tickling far back in his nostrils. He was going to — he was —

Eyes squeezed shut, his whole body contorted with effort, he raised his arm to begin the desperate race once more. His hand brushed against something — his kit, slung just above his waist. There were handkerchiefs in the kit, he recalled suddenly. And he remembered what the guide had said about Aurigean air.

He tugged the kit open, fumbled and found a handkerchief. He zipped open the closure of his helmet and tilted the helmet back. He brought up the handkerchief, and gave himself over to the spasm.

*H*e was startled by a hoarse boom, as if someone had scraped the strings of an amplified bull fiddle. He looked around, blinking, and discovered that the sound was coming from the Aurigean. The monster, with its tentacles tightly curled around the tip of its body, was scuttling into the corridor. As Weaver watched in confusion, it vanished, and a sheet of metal slid across the doorway.

More boomings came shortly from a source Weaver finally identified as a grille over the control panels. He took a step that way, then changed his mind and turned back toward the airlock.

Just as he reached the nearer airlock door, the farther one swung open and an instant torrent of wind thrust him outward.

Strangling, Weaver grabbed desperately at the door-frame as it went by. He swung with a sickening thud into the inner wall, but he hung on and pulled himself back inside.

The force of the wind was dropping rapidly; so was the air pressure. Ragged black blotches swam before Weaver's eyes. He fumbled with his helmet, trying to swing it back over his head; but it stubbornly remained where it was. The blow when he struck the airlock wall, he thought dimly — it must have bent the helmet so that it would not fit into its grooves.

He forced himself across the room, toward the faint gleam of the Aurigean control board — shaped like a double horseshoe it was, around the two lattice-topped stools, and bristling with levers, knobs and sliding panels. One of these, he knew, controlled the airlock. He slapped blindly at them, pulling, pushing, turning as many as he could reach. Then the floor reeled under him, and, as he fell toward it, changed into a soft grey endless mist. . . .

*W*hen he awoke, the airlock door was closed. His lungs were gratefully full of air. The Aurigean was nowhere to be seen; the door behind which he had disappeared was still closed.

Weaver got up, stripped off his spacesuit, and, by hammering with the sole of one of the boots, managed to straighten out the dent in the back of the helmet. He put the suit back on, then looked doubtfully at the control board. It wouldn't do to go on pulling things at random; he might cause some damage. Tentatively, he pushed a slide he remembered touching before. When nothing happened, he pushed it back. He tried a knob, then a lever.

The inner door of the airlock swung open.

Weaver marched into it, took one look through the viewport set in the outer door, and scrambled back out. He closed the airlock again, and thought a minute.

In the center of each horseshoe curve of the control board was a grey translucent disk, with six buttons under it. They might, Weaver thought, be television screens. He pressed the first button under one of them, and the screen lighted up. He pressed the second button, then all the others in turn.

They all showed him the same thing — the view he had seen from the viewport in the airlock: stars, and nothing but stars.

The Moon, incredibly, had disappeared. He was in space.

*H*is first thought, when he was able to think connectedly again, was to find the Aurigean and make him put things right. He tried all the remaining knobs and levers and buttons on the control board, reckless of consequences, until the door slid open again. Then he went down the corridor and found the Aurigean.

The creature was lying on the floor, with a turnip-shaped thing over its head, tubes trailing from it to an opened cabinet in the wall. It was dead — dead and decaying.

He searched the ship. He found storerooms, with cylinders and bales of stuff that looked as if it might possibly be food; he found the engine room, with great piles of outlandishly sculptured metal and winking lights and swinging meter needles. But he was the only living thing on board.

The view from all six directions — in the control room telescreens, and in the ship's direct-view ports alike — was exactly the same. The stars, like dandruff on Weaver's blue serge suit. No one of them, apparently, any nearer than the others. No way to tell which, if any of them, was his own.

The smell of the dead creature was all through the ship. Weaver closed his helmet against it; then, remembering that the air in his suit tank would not last forever, he lugged the corpse out to the airlock, closed the inner door on it, and opened the outer one.

It was hard for him to accept the obvious explanation of the Aurigean's death, but he finally came to it. He recalled something the guide had said about the Aurigeans' susceptibility to Earthly infections. That must have been it. That had been why the creature had bellowed and run to seal itself off from him. It was all his fault.

If he had not sneezed with his helmet open, the Aurigean would not be dead. He would not be marooned in space. And the other Aurigeans, down on Earth, would not be marooned there. Though they, he decided wistfully, would probably get home sooner or later. They knew where home was.

*A*s far as he could, he made himself master of the ship and its contents. He discovered, by arduous trial and error, which of the supposed foods in the storerooms he could eat safely, which would make him sick, and which were not foods at all. He found out which of the control board's knobs and levers controlled the engines, and he shut them off. He studied the universe around him, hoping to see some change.

After nearly a month, it happened. One star grew from a brilliant pinpoint to a tiny disk, and each time he awoke it was larger.

Weaver took counsel with himself, and pasted a small piece of transparent red tape over the place on the telescreen where the star appeared. He scratched a mark to show where the star was on each of three succeeding "days." The trail crawled diagonally down toward the bottom of the screen.

He knew nothing about astrogation; but he knew that if he were heading directly toward the star, it ought to stay in the same place on his screen. He turned on the engines and swung the steering arm downward. The star crawled toward the center of the screen, then went past. Weaver painstakingly brought it back; and so, in parsec-long zigzags, he held his course.

The star was now increasing alarmingly in brightness. It occurred to Weaver that he must be traveling with enormous speed, although he had no sensation of movement at all. There was a position on the scale around the steering arm that he thought would put the engines into reverse. He tried it, and now he scratched the apparent size of the star into the red tape. First it grew by leaps and bounds, then more slowly, then hardly at all. Weaver shut off the engines again, and waited.

The star had planets. He noted their passage in the telescreen, marked their apparent courses, and blithely set himself to land on the one that seemed to be nearest. He was totally ignorant of orbits; he simply centered his planet on the screen as he had done with the star, found that it was receding from him, and began to run it down.

He came in too fast the first time — tore through the atmosphere like a lost soul and frantically out again, sweating in the control room's sudden heat. He turned, out in space, and carefully adjusted his speed so that ship and planet drifted softly together. Gently, as if he had been doing this all his life. Weaver took the ship down upon a continent of rolling greens and browns, landed it without a jar — saw the landscape begin to tilt as he stepped into the airlock, and barely got outside before the ship rolled ten thousand feet down a gorge he had not noticed and smashed itself into a powdering of fragments.

Two days later, he began turning into a god.

II

*T*hey had put him into a kind of enclosed seat at the end of a long rotating arm, counter-weighted at the opposite side of the aircar proper, and the whole affair swung gently in an eccentric path, around and around, and up and down as the aircar moved very slowly forward through the village.

All the houses were faced with broad wooden balconies stained blood-red and turquoise, umber and yellow, gold and pale green; and all of these were crowded to bursting with the blue and white horny chests and the big-eyed faces of the bug things. Weaver swung in his revolving seat past first one level and another, and the twittering voices burst around him like the stars of a Fourth-of-July rocket.

This was the fifth village they had visited since the bug things had found him wandering in the mountains. At the first one, he had been probed, examined and twittered over interminably; then the aircar had arrived, they had strapped him into this ridiculous seat and begun what looked very much like a triumphal tour. Other aircars, without the revolving arm, preceded and followed him. The slowly floating cars and their riders were gay with varicolored streamers. Every now and then one of the bug things in the cars would raise a pistollike object to fire a pinkish streak that spread out, high in the air, and became a gently descending, diffusing cloud of rosy dust. And always the twittering rose and fell, rose and fell as Weaver revolved at the end of the swinging arm.

One had to remember, he reminded himself, that Earthly parallels did not necessarily apply. It was undignified, certainly, to be revolving like a child on a merry-go-round, while these crowds glared with bright alien eyes; but the important thing was that they had not once offered him any violence. They had not even put him into the absurd revolving seat by force; they had led him to it gently, with a great deal of gesturing and twittered explanation. And if their faces were almost nauseatingly unpleasant — with the constantly-moving complexity of parts that he had seen in live lobsters — well, that proved nothing except that they were not human. Later, perhaps, he could persuade them to wear masks. . . .

*I*t was a holiday; a great occasion — everything testified to that. The colored streamers, the clouds of rosy dust like sky-rockets, the crowds of people lined up to await him. And why not? Clearly, they had never before seen a man. He was unique, a personage to be honored: a visitor descended from the heavens, clothed in fire and glory. Like the Spaniards among the Aztecs, he thought.

Weaver began to feel gratified, his ego expanding. Experimentally, he waved to the massed ranks of bug things as he passed them. A new explosion of twittering broke out, and a forest of twiglike arms waved back at him. They seemed to regard him with happy awe.

"Thank you," said Weaver graciously. "Thank you. . . ."

In the morning, there were crowds massed outside the building where he had slept; but they did not put him into the aircar with the revolving arm again.

Instead, four new ones came into his room after he had eaten the strange red and orange fruits that were all of the bug diet he could stomach, and began to twitter very seriously at him, while pointing to various objects, parts of their bodies, the walls around them, and Weaver himself.

*A*fter awhile, Weaver grasped the idea that he was being instructed. He was willing to co-operate, but he did not suppose for a moment that he could master the birdlike sounds they made. Instead, he took an old envelope and a stub of pencil from his pocket and wrote the English word for each thing they pointed out. "OR-ANGE," he wrote — it was not an orange, but the color was the same, at any rate — "THORAX. WALL. MAN. MANDIBLES."

In the afternoon, they brought a machine with staring lenses and bright lights. Weaver guessed that he was being televised; he put a hand on the nearest bug thing's shoulder, and smiled for his audience.

Later, after he had eaten again, they went on with the language lesson. Now it was Weaver who taught, and they who learned. This, Weaver felt, was as it should be. These creatures were not men, he told himself; he would give himself no illusions on that score; but they might still be capable of learning many things that he had to teach. He could do a great deal of good, even if it turned out that he could never return to Earth.

He rather suspected that they had no spaceships. There was something about their life — the small villages, the slowly drifting aircars, the absence of noise and smell and dirt, that somehow did not fit with the idea of space travel. As soon as he was able, he asked them about it. No they had never traveled beyond their own planet. It was a great marvel; perhaps he could teach them how, sometime.

As their command of written English improved, he catechized them about themselves and their planet. The world, as he knew already, was much like Earth as to atmosphere, gravity and mean temperature. It occurred to him briefly that he had been lucky to hit upon such a world, but the thought did not stick; he had no way of knowing just how improbable his luck had been.

They themselves were, as he had thought, simple beings. They had a written history of some twelve thousand of their years, which he estimated to be about nine thousand of his. Their technical accomplishments, he had to grant, equaled Earth's and in some cases surpassed them. Their social organization was either so complex that it escaped him altogether, or unbelievably simple. They did not, so far as he could discover, have any political divisions. They did not make war.

They were egg-layers, and they controlled their population simply by means of hatching only as many eggs as were needed to replace their natural losses.

*J*ust when it first struck Weaver that he was their appointed ruler it would be hard to say. It began, perhaps, that afternoon in the aircar; or a few days later when he made his first timid request — for a house of his own. The request was eagerly granted, and he was asked how he would like the house constructed. Half timidly, he drew sketches of his own suburban home in Schenectady; and they built it, swarms of them working together, down to the hardwood floors and the pneumatic furniture and the picture moldings and the lamp-shades.

Or perhaps the idea crystallized when he asked to see some of their native dances, and within an hour the dancers assembled on his lawn — five hundred of them — and performed until sundown.

At, any rate, nothing could have been more clearly correct once he had grasped the idea. He was a Man, alone in a world of outlandish creatures. It was natural that he should lead; indeed, it was his duty. They were poor things, but they were malleable in his hands. It was a great adventure. Who knew how far he might not bring them?

Weaver embarked on a tour of the planet, taking with him two of the bug things as guides and a third as pilot and personal servant. Their names in their own tongue he had not bothered to ask; he had christened them Mark, Luke and John. All three now wrote and read English with fair proficiency; thus Weaver was well served.

The trip was entirely enjoyable. He was met everywhere by the same throngs, the same delight and enthusiasm as before; and between villages — there seemed to be nothing on the planet that could be called a city — the rolling green countryside, dotted with bosquets of yellow- and orange-flowered trees, was most soothing to the eye. Weaver noted the varieties of strangely shaped and colored plants, and the swarms of bright flying things, and began an abortive collection. He had to give it up, for the present: there were too many things to study. He looked forward to a few books to be compiled later, when he had time, for the guidance of Earthmen at some future date: *The Flora of Terranova, The Fauna of Terranova.* . . .

All that was for the distant future. Now he was chiefly concerned with the Terranovans themselves — how they lived, what they thought, what sort of primitive religion they had, and so on. He asked endless questions of his guides, and through them, of the villagers they met; and the more he learned, the more agitated he became.

"*B*ut this is monstrous," he wrote indignantly to Mark and Luke. They had just visited a house inhabited by seventeen males and twelve females — Weaver was now beginning to be able to distinguish the sexes — and he had inquired what their relations were. Mark had informed him calmly that they were husbands and wives; and when Weaver pointed out that the balance was uneven, had written, "No, not one to one. All to all. All husband and wife of each other."

Mark held Weaver's indignant message up to his eyes with one many-jointed claw, while his other three forelimbs gestured uncertainly. Finally he seized the note-pad and wrote, "Do not understand monstrous, please forgive. They do for more change, so not to make each other have tiredness."

Weaver frowned and wrote, "Does not your religion forbid this?"

Mark consulted in his own piping tongue with the other two. Finally he surrendered the note-pad to Luke, who wrote: "Do not understand religion to forbid, please excuse. With us many religion, some say spirits in flower, some say in wind and sun, some say in ground. Not say to do this, not to do that. With us all people the same, no one tell other what to do."

Weaver added another mental note to his already lengthy list: "Build churches."

He wrote: "Tell them this must stop."

Mark turned without hesitation to the silently attentive group, and translated. He turned back to Weaver and wrote, "They ask please, what to do now instead of the way they do?"

Weaver told him, "They must mate only one to one, and for life."

To his surprise, the translation of this was greeted by unmistakable twitterings of gladness. The members of the adulterous group turned to each other with excited gestures, and Weaver saw a pairing-off process begin, with much discussion.

He asked Mark about it later, as they were leaving the village. "How is it that they did this thing before — for more variety, as you say — and yet seem so glad to stop?"

Mark's answer was: "They very glad to do whatever thing you say. You bring them new thing, they very happy."

Weaver mused on this, contentedly on the whole, but with a small undigested kernel of uneasiness, until they reached the next village. Here he found a crowd of Terranovans of both sexes and all ages at a feast of something with a fearful stench. He asked what it was; Mark's answer had better not be revealed. Feeling genuinely sick with revulsion, Weaver demanded, "Why do they do such an awful thing? This is ten times worse than the other."

This time Mark answered without hesitation. "They do this like the other, for more change. Is not easy to learn to like, but they do, so not to make themselves have tiredness."

*T*here were three more such incidents before they reached the village where they were to sleep that night; and Weaver lay awake in his downy bed, staring at the faint shimmer of reflected starlight on the carved roof-beams, and meditating soberly on the unexpected, the appalling magnitude of the task he had set himself.

From this, he came to consider that small dark kernel of doubt. It was of course dreadful to find that his people were so wholly corrupt, but that at least was understandable. What he did not understand was the reason they could be so easily weaned from their wickedness. It left him feeling a little off-balance, like a man who has hurled himself at his enemy and found him suddenly not there. This reminded him of ju-jitsu, and this in turn of the ancient Japanese — to whom, indeed, his Terranovans seemed to have many resemblances. Weaver's uneasiness increased. Savage peoples were notoriously devious — they smiled and then thrust knives between your ribs.

He felt a sudden prickling coldness at the thought. It was improbable, it was fantastic that they would go to such lengths to gratify his every wish if they meant to kill him, he told himself; and then he remembered the Dionysian rites, and a host of other, too-similar parallels. The king for a day or a year, who ruled as an absolute monarch, and then was sacrificed —

And, Weaver remembered with a stab of panic, usually eaten.

He had been on Terranova for a little over a month by the local calendar. What was his term of office to be — two months? Six? A year, ten years?

*H*e slept little that night, woke late in the morning with dry, irritated eyes and a furred mouth, and spent a silent day, inspecting each new batch of natives without comment, and shivering inwardly at each motion of the clawed arms of Mark, Luke or John. Toward evening he came out of his funk at last, when it occurred to him to ask about weapons.

He put the query slyly, wording it as if it were a matter of general interest only, and of no great importance. Were they familiar with machines that killed, and if so, what varieties did they have?

At first Mark did not understand the question. He replied that their machines did not kill, that very long ago they had done so but that the machines were much better now, very safe and not harmful to anyone. "Then," wrote Weaver carefully, "you have no machines which are made for the purpose of killing?"

Mark, Luke and John discussed this with every evidence of excitement. At last Mark wrote, "This very new idea to us."

"But do you have in this world no large, dangerous animals which must be killed? How do you kill those things which you eat?"

"No dangerous animals. We kill food things, but not use machines. Give some things food which make them die. Give some no food, so they die. Kill some with heat. Some eat alive."

Weaver winced with distaste when he read this last, and was about to write, "This must stop." But he thought of oysters, and decided to reserve judgment.

After all, it had been foolish of him to be frightened last night. He had been carried away by a chance comparison which, calmly considered, was superficial and absurd. These people were utterly peaceful — in fact, spineless.

He wrote, "Take the aircar up farther, so that I can see this village from above."

He signaled John to stop when they had reached a height of a few hundred feet. From this elevation, he could see the village spread out beneath him like an architect's model — the neat cross-hatching of narrow streets separating the hollow curves of rooftops, dotted with the myriad captive balloons launched in honor of his appearance.

The village lay in the gentle hollow of a wide valley, surrounded by the equally gentle slopes of hills. To his right, it followed the bank of a fair-sized river; in the other three directions the checkered pattern ended in a careless, irregular outline and was replaced by the larger pattern of cultivated fields.

It was a good site — the river for power, sanitation and transportation, the hills for a sheltered climate. He saw suddenly, in complete, sharp detail, how it would be.

"The trip is over," he wrote with sudden decision. "We will stay here, and build a city."

III

*T*he most difficult part was the number of things that he had to learn. There was no trouble about anything he wanted done by others; he simply commanded, and that was the end of it. But the mass of knowledge about the Terranovans and their world before he came appalled him not only by its sheer bulk but by its intricacy, the unexplained gaps, the contradictions. For a long time after the founding of New Washington — later New Jerusalem — he was still bothered a little by doubt. He wanted to learn all that there was to learn about the Terranovans, so that finally he would understand them completely and the doubt would be gone.

Eventually he confessed to himself that the task was impossible. He was forty-seven years old; he had perhaps thirty years ahead of him, and it was not as if he were able to devote them solely to study. There was the written history of the Terranovans, which covered minutely a period of nine thousand years — though not completely; there were periods and places which seemed to have left no adequate records of themselves. The natives had no reasonable explanation of this phenomenon; they simply said that the keeping of histories sometimes went out of fashion.

Then there was the biology of the Terranovans and the countless other organisms of the planet — simply to catalogue them and give them English names, as he had set out to do, would have occupied him the rest of his lifetime.

There was the complex and puzzling field of social relations — here again everything seemed to be in unaccountable flux, even though the overall pattern remained the same and seemed as rigid as any primitive people's. There was physics, which presented exasperating difficulties of translation; there was engineering, there was medicine, there was economics. . . .

*W*hen he finally gave it up, it was not so much because of the simple arithmetical impossibility of the job as because he realized that it didn't matter. For a time he had been tempted away from the logical attitude toward these savages of his — a foolish weakness of the sort that had given him that ridiculous hour or two, when, he now dimly recalled, he had been afraid of the Terranovans — afraid, of all things, that they were fattening him for the sacrifice!

Whereas it was clear enough, certainly, that the *former* state of the Terranovans, their incomprehensible society and language and customs, simply had no practical importance. He was changing all that. When he was through, they would be what he had made them, no more and no less.

It was strange, looking back, to realize how little he had seen of his destiny, there at the beginning. Timid little man, he thought half in amusement, half contemptuously: nervous and fearful, seeing things *small.* Build me a house, like the one I had in Schenectady!

They had built him a palace — no, a *temple* — and a city; and they were building him a world. A planet that would be his to the last atom when it was done; a corner of the universe that was Algernon James Weaver.

He recalled that in the beginning he had felt almost like these creatures' servant — "public servant," he had thought, with self-righteous lukewarm, pleasure. He had seen himself as one who built for others — the more virtuous because those others were not even men.

But it was not he who built. *They* built, and for him.

It was strange, he thought again, that he should not have seen it from the first. For it was perfectly clear and all of a pattern.

The marriage laws. *Thou shalt not live in adultery.*

The dietary laws. *Thou shalt not eat that which is unclean.*

And the logical concomitant, the law of worship. *Thou shalt have no gods before Me.*

*T*he apostles . . . Mark, Luke and John. Later, Matthew, Philip, Peter, Simon, Andrew, James, Bartholomew and Thomas.

He had a feeling that something was wrong with the list besides the omission of Judas — unluckily, he had no Bible — but it was really an academic question. They were *his* apostles, not that Other's.

The pattern repeated itself, he thought, but with variations.

He understood now why he had shelved the project of Christianizing the natives, although one of his first acts had been to abolish their pagan sects. He had told himself at first that it was best to wait until he had put down from memory the salient parts of the Holy Bible — Genesis, say, the better-known Psalms, and a condensed version of the Gospels; leaving out all the begats, and the Jewish tribal history, and awkward things like the Songs of Solomon. (*Thy mandibles are like pomegranates* . . . no, it wouldn't do).

And, of course, he had never found time to wrack his brains for the passages that eluded him. But all that had been merely a subterfuge to soothe his conscience, while he slowly felt his way into his new role.

Now, it was almost absurdly simple. He was writing his own holy book — or rather, Luke, Thomas, and a corps of assistants were putting it together from his previous utterances, to be edited by him later.

The uneasy rustling of chitinous arms against white robes recalled him from his meditation. The swarm of priests, altar boys, and the rest of his retinue was still gathered around him, waiting until he should deign to notice them again. Really, God thought with annoyance, this woolgathering — at such a moment!

*T*he worshippers were massed in the Temple. A low, excited twittering rose from them as He appeared and walked into the beam of the spotlight.

The dark lenses of television cameras were focused on Him from every part of the balcony at the rear of the hall. The microphones were ready. Weaver walked forward as the congregation knelt, and waited an impressive moment before He spread His hands in the gesture that meant, "Rise, my children." Simon, previously coached, translated. The congregation rose again, rustling, and then was still.

At a signal from Simon, the choir began a skirling and screeching which the disciples warranted to be music — religious music, composed to fit the requirements He had laid down. Weaver endured it, thinking that some changes must come slowly.

The hymn wailed to an end, and Weaver gripped the lectern, leaning carefully forward toward the microphones. "My children," He began, and waited for Solomon's twittering translation. "You have sinned greatly —" Twitter. "— and in many ways." Twitter. "But I have come among you —" Twitter. "— to redeem your sins —" Twitter. "— and make them as though they had never been." Twitter.

He went on to the end, speaking carefully and sonorously. It was not a long sermon, but He flattered Himself that it was meaty. At the end of it He stepped back a pace, and folded His arms, in their long white-silk sleeves, across His chest.

Simon took over now, and so far as Weaver could judge, he did well. He recited a litany which Weaver had taught him, indicating by gestures that the congregation was to repeat after him every second speech. The low chirping welled from the hall; a comforting, warming sound, almost like the responses of a human congregation. Weaver felt tears welling to His eyes, and He restrained Himself from weeping openly only by a gigantic effort. After all, He was a god of wrath; but the love which swept toward Him at this moment was a powerful thing to gainsay.

*W*hen it was all over, He went back to His sanctum, dismissed all His retinue except His regular assistants, and removed the ceremonial robes.

"The people responded well," He said. "I am pleased."

Simon said, "They will work hard to please You, Master. You bring great happiness to them."

"That is well," said Weaver. He sat down behind His great desk, while the others stood attentively below Him, in the sunken fore-section of the sanctum. "What business have you for Me today?"

"There is the matter of the novel, Master," said Mark. He stepped forward, mounted the single step to Weaver's daïs, and laid a sheaf of papers on the desk. "This is a preliminary attempt which one called Peter Smith has made with my unworthy help."

"I will read it later," Weaver told him. It was poor stuff, no doubt — what else could one expect? — but it was a start. He would tell them what was wrong with it, and they would try again.

Literary criticism, armaments, tariffs, manners — there was no end to it. "What else?"

Luke stepped forward. "The plans for the large weapons You commanded Your servants to design,

Master." He put three large sheets of parchment on the desk.

Weaver looked at the neat tracery on the first, and frowned. "You may come near Me," He said. "Show Me how these are meant to operate."

Luke pointed to the first drawing. "This is the barrel of the weapon, Master," he said. "As You commanded, it is rifled so that the missile will spin. Here the missile is inserted at the breech, according to Your direction. Here is the mechanism which turns and aims the weapon, as You commanded. It is shown in greater detail on this second sheet. . . . And here, on the third, is the missile itself. It is hollow and filled with explosive powder, as You ordered, and there is in the tip a device which will attract it to the target."

Weaver gravely nodded. "Has it been tested?"

"In models only, Master. If You direct, the construction will begin at once."

"Good. Proceed. How many of these can you make for Me within a month?"

Luke hesitated. "Few, Master. At first all must be done by hand methods. Later it will be possible to make many at a time — fifty, or even a hundred in one month — but for the first two or three months, Master, two weapons in a month is all that Your unworthy servants can do."

"Very well," said Weaver. "See to it."

*H*e turned and examined the large globe of the planet which stood on His desk. Here was another product of His genius; the Terranovans had scarcely had maps worthy of the name before His Coming.

The three major continents trailed downward like fleshy leaves from the north pole; He had called them America, Europe and Asia, and they were so lettered on the globe. In the southern hemisphere, besides the tips of Europe and Asia and fully a third of America, there was a fourth continent, shaped rather like a hat, which He had called Australia. There was no Africa on Terranova, but that was small loss: Weaver had never thought highly of Africa.

The planet itself, according to the experts who had been assigned the problem, was a little more than ten thousand miles in diameter. The land area, Weaver thought, probably amounted to more than fifty million square miles. It was a great deal to defend; but it must be done.

"Here is your next assignment," He told Luke. "Put a team to work on selecting and preparing sites for these guns, when they are built. There must be one in every thousand square miles. . . ."

Luke bowed and took the plans away.

. . . For otherwise, Weaver thought somberly, another ship might land, some day. And how could I trust these children not to *welcome* it?

Sunlight gleamed brilliantly from the broad, white-marble plaza beyond the tall portico. Looking through the windows, He could see the enormous block of stone in the center of the plaza, and the tiny robot aircar hovering near it, and the tiny ant-shapes of the crowd on the opposite side. Beyond, the sky was a clear, faultless blue.

"Are you ready now, Master?" asked Luke.

Weaver tested His limbs. They were rigid and almost without sensation; He could not move them so much as the fraction of an inch. Even His lips were as stiff as that marble outside. Only the fingers of His right hand, clutching a pen, felt as if they belonged to Him.

A metal frame supported a note-pad where His hand could reach it. Then he wrote, "Yes. Proceed with the statue."

Luke was holding a tiny torpedo-shaped object that moved freely at the end of a long, jointed metal arm. He moved it tentatively toward Weaver's left shoulder. Outside, the hovering aircar duplicated the motion: the grinder at its tip bit with a screech into the side of the huge stone.

Weaver watched, feeling no discomfort; the drug Luke had injected was working perfectly. Luke moved the pantograph pointer, again and again, until it touched Weaver's robed body. With every motion, the aircar bored a tunnel into the stone to the exact depth required, and backed out again. Slowly a form was beginning to emerge.

The distant screech of the grinder was muffled and not unpleasant. Weaver felt a trifle sleepy.

The top of one extended arm was done. The aircar moved over and began the other, leaving the head still buried in stone.

After this, Weaver thought, He could rest. His cities were built, His church founded, His guns built and tested, His people trained. The Terranovans were as civilized as He could make them in one generation.

They had literary societies, newsstands, stock markets, leisure and working classes, baseball leagues, armies. . . . They had had to give up their barbaric comfort, of course; so much the better. Life was real, life was earnest — Weaver had taught them that.

The mechanism of His government ran smoothly; it would continue to run, with only an occasional guiding touch. This was His last major task. The monument.

Something to remember Me by, He thought drowsily. Myself in stone, long after I am gone. That will keep them to My ways, even if they should be tempted. To them I will still be here, standing over them, gigantic, imperishable.

They will still have something to worship.

Stone dust was obscuring the figure now, glittering in the sunlight. Luke undercut a huge block of the stone and it fell, turning lazily, and crashed on the pavement. Robot tractors darted out to haul the pieces away.

Weaver was glad it was Luke whose hand was guiding the pantograph, not one of the bright, efficient younger generation. They had been together a long time, Luke and He. Almost ten years. He knew Luke as if he were a human being; *understood* him as if he were a person. And Luke knew Him better than any of the rest; knew His smiles and His frowns, all His moods.

It had been a good life. He had done all the things He set out to do, and He had done them in His own time and His own way. At this distance, it was almost impossible to believe that He had once been a little man among billions of others, conforming to their patterns, doing what was expected of Him.

His free hand was growing tired from holding the pen. When all the rest was done, Luke would freeze that hand also, and then it would be only a minute or so until he could inject the antidote. He scribbled idly, "Do you remember the old days, before I came, Luke?"

"Very well, Master," said the apostle. "But it seems a long time ago."

Yes, Weaver told Himself contentedly; just what I was thinking. We understand each other, Luke and I. He wrote, "Things are very different now, eh?"

"Very different, Master. You made many changes. The people are very grateful to You."

He could see the broad outlines of the colossal figure now: the arms, in their heavy ecclesiastical sleeves, outstretched in benediction, the legs firmly planted. But the bowed head was still a rough, featureless mass of stone, not yet shaped.

"Do you know," Weaver wrote, on impulse, "that when I first came, I thought for a time that you were savages who might want to eat Me?"

That would startle Luke, He thought. But Luke said, "We all wanted to, very much. But that would have been foolish, Master. Then we would not have had all the other things. And besides, there would not have been enough of You for all."

The aircar screeched, driving a tunnel along the edge of the parted vestments.

God felt a cold wind down the corridor of time. He had been that close, after all. It was only because the natives had been cold-bloodedly foresighted that He was still alive. The idea infuriated Him, and somehow He was still afraid.

He wrote, "You never told me this. You will all do a penance for it."

Luke was dabbing the pointer carefully at the bald top of Weaver's head. His horny, complicated face was unpleasantly close, the mandibles unpleasantly big even behind his mouth veil.

Luke said, "We will, very gladly . . . except that perhaps the new ones will not like it."

Weaver felt bewildered. In one corner of His mind He felt a tiny darkness unfolding: the kernel of doubt, forgotten so long, but there all the time. Growing larger now, expanding to a ragged, terrifying shape.

He wrote, "What do you mean? Who are 'the new ones'?"

Luke said, "We did not tell You. We knew You would not like it. A spaceship landed in Asia two months ago. There are three people in it. One is sick, but we believe the other two will live. They are very funny people, Master."

The pantograph pointer moved down the side of God's nose and another wedge of stone fell in the plaza.

"They have three long legs, and a very little body, and a head with one eye in front and one behind. Also they have very funny ideas. They are horrified at the way we live, and they are going to change it all around."

Weaver's fingers jerked uncontrollably, and the words wavered across the page. "I don't understand. I don't understand."

"I hope You are not angry. Master," said Luke. "We are very grateful to You. When You came, we were desperately bored. There had been no new thing for more than seven thousand years, since the last ship came from space. You know that we have not much imagination. We tried to invent new things for ourselves, but we could never think of anything so amusing as the ones You gave us. We will always remember You with gratitude."

The pantograph was tracing Weaver's eyelids, and then the unfeeling eyes themselves.

*B*ut all things must end," said Luke. "Now we have these others, who do not like what you have done, so we cannot worship you anymore. And anyway, some of the people are growing tired. It has been ten years. A long time."

One thought pierced through the swirling fear in Weaver's mind. The guns, built with so much labor, the enormous guns that could throw a shell two hundred miles. The crews, manning them night and day to destroy the first ship that came in from space. And they had never meant to use them!

Anger fought with caution. He felt peculiarly helpless now, locked up in his own body like a prison. "What are you going to do?" he scrawled.

"Nothing that will hurt, Master," said Luke. "You remember, I told you long ago, we had no machines for killing before you came. We used other things, like this drug which paralyzes. You will feel no pain."

Algernon Weaver's hand, gripping the pen as a drowning man holds to a stave, was moving without his volition. It was scrawling in huge letters, over and over, "No no no. . . ."

"It is too bad we cannot wait," said Luke, "but it has to be done before the new ones get here. They would not like it, probably."

He let the pointer go, and it hung where he had left it. With two jointed claws he seized Weaver's hand and straightened it out to match the other, removing the pen. With a third claw he thrust a slender needle under the skin. Instantly the hand was as rigid as the rest of Weaver's body. Weaver felt as if the last door had been slammed, the telephone wires cut, the sod thrown on the coffin.

"This is the way we have decided," said Luke. "It is a shame, because perhaps these new ones will not be as funny as you, after all. But it is the way we have decided."

He took up the pantograph pointer again.

*I*n the plaza, the aircar ground at the huge stone head, outlining the stern mouth, the resolute, bearded jaw. Helplessly, Weaver returned the stare of that remorseless, brooding face: the face of a conqueror.

www.ingramcontent.com/pod-product-compliance
Lightning Source LLC
Chambersburg PA
CBHW031903170626
46807CB00004B/1879